I0551491

DEDICATION

To my mother, Sandra Joy,

Your love, faith, and unwavering support have been a guiding light in my life.

You have shown me the beauty of faith, the power of perseverance, and the depth of God's grace.

This book is a reflection of the truth you instilled in me—the truth that God's plan is perfect, His promises are sure, and His return is near.

May this work honor your faith and the legacy of wisdom and love you have given me.

With love and gratitude,
Eric

FROM THE AUTHOR

What do you do when anxiety or stress overwhelms you?

For me, I've made it a priority to study, research, and seek understanding. In times of uncertainty, I turn to God's Word, prophecy, and history to find clarity and peace.

My son is at that age where he is making his own choices, torn between different worldviews, searching for truth. As a father, I know that our days are numbered, and while I hope to always be there to guide him, I also know that if I am not, he will never be without answers—because he will always have his Bible and the foundation that I have instilled in him.

And for the days when he misses me, when life feels uncertain, or when he simply has a yearning to go deeper in his faith, he will also have my thoughts and beliefs in these books that I have published. My hope is that they serve as a reminder of the truth, a resource to turn to when the world seems chaotic, and a guide to help him navigate life through the lens of Scripture.

That is my wish—not just for him, but for each of you.

We are living in extraordinary times. The world is changing at an unprecedented pace, and more than ever, people are searching for answers. I wrote this book because I believe those answers have already been given to us—through prophecy, through history, and through the unshakable truth of God's Word.

I encourage you not just to read this book but to search the Scriptures for yourself. Let this book be a guide, but let the Bible be your foundation.

If you're reading this, you were meant to. There are no accidents with God.

My prayer is that as you turn these pages, you will find encouragement, wisdom, and the reassurance that He has been in control from the very beginning—and He always will be.

INTRODUCTION: THE STORY ALREADY WRITTEN

The world as we know it is on the edge of eternity.

The signs are everywhere—**wars and rumors of wars, nations rising against nations, earthquakes, famines, lawlessness increasing, and deception spreading like wildfire.** The world grows darker by the day, and many sense that **something is coming.**

Yet, for those who look to Scripture, none of this is a surprise.

God has already revealed **the entire timeline of human history,** from **the first breath of creation to the final establishment of His eternal Kingdom.** He has given us **the blueprint of the ages,** recorded in **prophecies that are unfolding before our very eyes.**

And the clock is nearing midnight.

WHY THIS BOOK?

7000 Years is not just a study of prophecy—it is an invitation to **see history through God's eyes**. It follows a pattern set from the very beginning, revealing how:

- **The first 6,000 years of human history** reflect **six days of labor**—a time of sin, redemption, and preparation.

- **The final 1,000 years** will be a **Sabbath rest**, when Christ rules and reigns as King.

- **Each major biblical event foreshadows a greater fulfillment yet to come.**

Throughout Scripture, God has revealed that **His plan follows the divine pattern of seven**—just as He **created the world in six days and rested on the seventh** (Genesis 2:2-3), He has ordained **six thousand years of human history followed by a thousand-year reign of Christ** (Revelation 20:4).

This book will take you through the **water, the blood, and the fire** —three key stages of history that lead us to the **final chapter of time**.

It is a journey through **creation, judgment, redemption, and restoration**.

And, like all great stories, it has an ending.

WHERE ARE WE NOW?

We are living at the very end of the **6,000-year timeline**.

The pieces are in place for the final prophetic events to unfold.

The **nation of Israel has been reborn** (Isaiah 66:8).

Global systems of control are being prepared for the Antichrist (Revelation 13:16-17).

The **world is calling for a false peace** (1 Thessalonians 5:3).

And **knowledge is increasing at an exponential rate** (Daniel 12:4).

Yet, **before the final judgments begin, a great event must first take place—the Rapture of the Church** (1 Thessalonians 4:16-17).

This book is written to prepare you for what is coming.

A PERSONAL INVITATION

Prophecy is not about fear—it is about hope.

If you are reading this, you are being given an opportunity.

An opportunity to **understand God's timeline**.
An opportunity to **see the signs**.
An opportunity to **be ready**.

The King is coming soon.

The question is—**will you be ready when He does?**

Turn the page, and let the **7000-year story unfold before you**.

The final chapter is about to begin.

OPENING SCRIPTURE

"BUT, BELOVED, DO NOT FORGET THIS ONE THING, THAT WITH THE LORD ONE DAY IS AS A THOUSAND YEARS, AND A THOUSAND YEARS AS ONE DAY."
— 2 PETER 3:8 (NKJV)

CHAPTER 1: THE ETERNAL AUTHOR

T he sun dipped below the horizon, painting the sky in hues of crimson and gold. On the edge of a small town, nestled between rolling hills and a glimmering river, stood an ancient library that seemed untouched by time. The scent of aged parchment filled the air, and the faint flicker of candles illuminated the room. It was here that Adrian first encountered the book that would change everything.

Adrian was a seeker—though he wouldn't have described himself that way. To him, life was a series of disconnected events, random and without purpose. Yet, a nagging sense of emptiness drove him to explore the forgotten corners of his world. Tonight, his search brought him to the library, a place he hadn't visited in years.

"Looking for something specific?" asked a voice, startling him.

Adrian turned to find an elderly librarian with sharp, inquisitive eyes that seemed to peer into his very soul. "I'm not sure," Adrian admitted, running his fingers through his disheveled hair. "Maybe something… meaningful."

The librarian nodded knowingly and disappeared behind a shelf, only to return moments later with a dusty, leather-bound tome. Its title, *The Story Written Before Time*, was etched in golden script.

"What is this?" Adrian asked, hesitating as he took the book.

"A story," the librarian replied. "But not just any story—it's the story of everything."

Curiosity won over caution, and Adrian settled into a corner of the library. As he opened the book, the words seemed to glow faintly, as if alive.

In the beginning, God created the heavens and the earth.

The sentence reverberated in his mind, accompanied by a strange warmth in his chest. The pages began to recount a narrative that felt both ancient and deeply personal. It spoke of an Author who had crafted a perfect world, only to see it fractured by rebellion.

Adrian's thoughts drifted to his own life—broken relationships, mistakes he couldn't undo, and dreams that had crumbled. The parallels were undeniable, and he felt an inexplicable pull to keep reading.

A Plan Beyond Time

The book described a plan set in motion before the foundation of the world—a timeline spanning seven days, each representing a thousand years. The first two days told of a world cleansed by water, a divine reset after humanity's corruption.

Adrian paused, his mind swirling. *Seven days? A thousand years each?* He flipped ahead, skimming passages about a second great event—a cleansing by blood—and a final age of fire and restoration. The narrative was vast, weaving history and prophecy together with unsettling precision.

"Every generation carries whispers of judgment, redemption, and restoration," the book declared. "Nothing in history is random. It is all part of the Author's story."

The Encounter

As the night deepened, Adrian felt the weight of the story pressing upon him. It wasn't just a tale—it was an invitation. The final chapter loomed, and the question lingered: *Are you ready?*

The librarian reappeared as Adrian closed the book. "What did you think?"

"It feels... real," Adrian said, his voice barely above a whisper. "Like it's about me."

The librarian smiled gently. "Perhaps it is. The story isn't finished, you know. It's still being written—one life at a time."

Adrian left the library that night with the book tucked under his arm, unaware that his journey had only just begun. The narrative had awakened something in him, a spark of hope and a hunger for truth. As he stepped into the crisp night air, he couldn't shake the feeling that he was standing on the edge of eternity, his own chapter waiting to unfold.

And so, the first page of his story began.

CHAPTER 2: WHISPERS
OF THE PAST

Adrian sat at his small wooden desk, the book resting before him like a relic from another world. The moonlight streaming through his window cast an otherworldly glow on the leather cover. He hadn't been able to sleep, the words of the book echoing in his mind, beckoning him to continue.

He opened it again, and the narrative seemed to flow as if the story itself wanted to be heard.

The Days Of Water

"In the beginning, the world was perfect, but perfection is fragile in the hands of free will," the book began, weaving a tale of creation, beauty, and betrayal. Adrian could picture the garden described—lush and vibrant, untouched by decay. Yet, it didn't last. A single choice changed everything, introducing a fracture that rippled through all of creation.

The story shifted to Noah, a man who lived in a world teetering on the brink of destruction. Humanity's corruption was total, its rebellion against the Author unabashed. Adrian could almost hear the mocking laughter as Noah built the ark, hammering away at a vessel of salvation while the world celebrated its descent into chaos.

The words described a flood unlike anything the earth had

ever seen, a cleansing by water. The imagery was vivid—waves crashing, skies weeping, and silence enveloping the world as the waters receded. Yet, amid the destruction was hope. Noah and his family emerged into a renewed world, a promise of mercy written in the colors of the rainbow.

Adrian's chest tightened. The flood wasn't just an event—it was a message, a reflection of his own life. How often had he ignored warnings, drifting further into the storm until only a miracle could pull him back?

A Message From The Past

Adrian turned the page, his heart racing. A new section began, not recounting history but addressing the reader directly.

"What of your life, traveler? Have the storms grown unbearable? Have you heard the call to prepare an ark of faith, or have you scoffed at the thought? The Author's hand is steady, but the door will not remain open forever."

He closed the book abruptly, his breathing uneven. It was as though the words had been written for him, speaking directly to his hidden fears and failures. He thought of the decisions he had made—paths taken out of pride or fear, relationships shattered by anger or neglect. The flood wasn't just ancient history. It was a reflection of the cleansing he desperately needed.

The night stretched on as Adrian wrestled with the story. He felt exposed, as if the book had laid bare the deepest corners of his soul. Yet, for the first time, he didn't feel alone in his struggles. The Author's presence seemed to linger in the room, unseen but undeniably real.

The Call

Morning came, but Adrian couldn't shake the weight of the book's message. He needed answers, someone to help him make sense of the overwhelming narrative. Without hesitation, he returned to the library.

The librarian greeted him with a knowing smile. "I had a feeling you'd be back."

Adrian placed the book on the counter, his voice firm. "I need to know more. What is this? Who wrote it?"

The librarian gestured for him to sit. "This story is as old as time, yet it's new for everyone who reads it. The Author is closer than you think, and His story isn't finished—not for you, not for anyone."

Adrian leaned forward, desperation creeping into his voice. "But what does it mean for me? Why do I feel like it's speaking directly to my life?"

The librarian's eyes softened. "Because it is. The Author knows every page of your story, Adrian. And He's offering you a chance to let Him write the next chapter. But it's a choice only you can make."

A Turning Point

Adrian left the library with more questions than answers, but for the first time in years, he felt a glimmer of hope. The story had drawn him in, challenging him to confront the chaos of his past and embrace the possibility of a new beginning.

As he walked home, the clouds began to part, revealing a brilliant blue sky. The promise of a rainbow lingered on the horizon, a reminder of the Author's faithfulness. Adrian knew he wasn't ready for the journey ahead, but perhaps readiness wasn't the point. The Author's hand was steady, and Adrian was beginning to trust that his story was far from over.

Little did he know, the days of water were only the beginning. The next chapter would take him deeper into the mystery, where blood and fire would unveil truths he had never imagined.

CHAPTER 3: THE BLOOD AND THE COVENANT

The night air was crisp as Adrian walked the dimly lit streets, his mind still tangled in the echoes of the book. The flood—the cleansing by water—had left him with a lingering sense of unease. It wasn't just about history; it was about something deeper, something personal.

What came next?

He clutched the book under his arm, its leather cover now familiar beneath his fingertips. The flood had wiped the world clean once before, but the words of the book hinted at something greater still. Water could cleanse the earth, but it could not change the heart of man.

He needed answers.

Without hesitation, he made his way back to the library.

The Librarian's Lesson

The old librarian was there, as if he had been waiting. He didn't look surprised to see Adrian again. Instead, he simply motioned toward a seat across from him, a warm cup of tea already placed on the table.

"You've seen the waters," the librarian said, eyes gleaming in the candlelight. "Now you must understand the blood."

Adrian furrowed his brow. "What do you mean?"

The librarian slid the book toward him, flipping it open to a section Adrian had not yet read. The pages whispered as they turned, the golden script shimmering faintly in the light.

"Water cleansed the world," the librarian explained, tapping a passage with his finger. "But it was never enough. The corruption of man was deeper than the surface. Another sacrifice was needed —one that would reach the very soul."

Adrian's gaze fell upon the passage.

The Blood Of The Lamb

It was the fullness of time when the covenant was sealed. The Author had set the stage long ago, weaving a promise through the generations. A promise that one would come—not with sword or fire, but with blood. A sacrifice. A Lamb.

The words sent a chill down Adrian's spine. He could almost see the ancient lands unfolding before him—the weary figure of Abraham walking beneath a starlit sky, the distant glow of torches flickering against the stone of an altar.

"Abraham," he murmured.

The librarian nodded. "A covenant sealed in blood. He was given a promise—that through him, all nations would be blessed. But that promise came at a cost."

Adrian watched as the words on the page shifted before him, drawing him into the story.

The Night Of The Covenant

The sky was dark, void of stars. Abraham stood in the silence, his heart pounding in his chest. He had obeyed, had followed the Voice that called him from his homeland, had trusted in the promise of descendants as numerous as the stars.

But tonight was different.

The animals lay before him, their blood staining the ground. He had divided them as commanded, preparing for a covenant that he barely understood.

And then it came.

Darkness.

A terror unlike any other fell upon him, and suddenly, the world seemed to shift. A smoking firepot and a blazing torch passed between the pieces, sealing the promise in a way that Abraham could not—would not—fully comprehend.

A covenant not of man's making, but of God's alone.

Adrian's breath caught in his throat as the scene faded from his mind, the book returning to its stillness.

The Shadow Of The Cross

"The promise was given," the librarian said softly. "But the true fulfillment would not come for thousands of years. The blood of bulls and goats could never take away sin. They were only shadows."

Adrian felt his fingers tighten around the book's edges.

"And then... He came."

The librarian's voice was barely above a whisper, but the weight of his words filled the room.

The words on the page glowed once more, and Adrian was drawn into the next scene.

The Hill Of Sacrifice

It was different from the covenant of Abraham.

This time, the altar was a hill.

The fire of God's presence was absent, replaced by the burning sun overhead. The blood was not of animals, but of a man— beaten, broken, nailed to the wood.

The Lamb had come.

Adrian's heart pounded as he read the words:

"Behold, the Lamb of God, who takes away the sin of the world."

He could see it—the agony, the darkness that covered the land, the moment when the veil tore from top to bottom. The covenant was completed, not with fire and smoke, but with a single cry:

"It is finished."

The book trembled in his hands.

The Invitation

Adrian shut the book, breathing heavily. He could feel it now —this wasn't just history. It wasn't just prophecy. It was an invitation.

"Why is this hitting me so hard?" he asked, his voice hoarse.

The librarian gave him a knowing look. "Because the covenant isn't just about the past. It's about you."

Adrian swallowed hard. "What do you mean?"

The librarian leaned forward. "The flood was about cleansing. But the blood... the blood is about redemption. The Author is offering you a place in His story, Adrian. A new beginning. But you must choose."

Adrian looked down at the book, the weight of it pressing into his hands.

The first covenant had been sealed in blood. The second had been fulfilled in blood.

And now, he stood at the crossroads of his own story.

Would he accept the sacrifice?

Would he allow the Author to write his next chapter?

The room was silent, save for the flickering of the candlelight.

Adrian closed his eyes.

And for the first time, he whispered a prayer.

CHAPTER 4: THE FIRE AND THE CALL

The wind howled through the trees as Adrian stepped out of the library, the weight of the book pressing against his chest. His mind swirled with the echoes of the past—the flood, the covenant, the sacrifice of the Lamb.

But there was something more.

Something unfinished.

He turned his gaze upward, watching as the clouds drifted across the moonlit sky. The librarian's words still rang in his ears:

"The covenant isn't just about the past. It's about you."

A shiver ran down his spine. He had seen the water. He had glimpsed the blood. But deep in his soul, he knew that something was coming—something that would shake the very foundations of everything he believed.

The book had shown him the past.

Now, it would reveal the future.

The Fire Foretold

Adrian sat at his desk, the book open before him, candlelight flickering against the pages. His fingers traced the golden script as he read:

"Water cleansed the earth. Blood redeemed the people. But fire... fire will purify all things."

His pulse quickened as the words shifted, transporting him into another vision. The landscape was unfamiliar—harsh, barren, trembling under the weight of unseen forces. The sky was dark, churning with a storm that carried no rain, only fire.

A voice echoed through the chaos:

"For behold, the day is coming, burning like an oven..."

Adrian's breath hitched as he watched. Mountains trembled, cities crumbled, and flames devoured the land. It was not mere destruction—it was transformation.

He turned the page.

"The earth groans, waiting for the fulfillment of all things. The fire is coming, not to destroy, but to refine."

The words were stark, yet filled with hope.

Adrian pressed a hand to his forehead, trying to steady his thoughts. Fire—was it judgment, or was it something more?

His eyes scanned the next passage.

The Baptism Of Fire

"John came with water. The Lamb came with blood. But the One who is coming will baptize with Spirit and fire."

The scene shifted, and Adrian found himself standing at the banks of the Jordan River. He could see him—the wild prophet clothed in camel's hair, eyes ablaze with purpose.

John the Baptist.

His voice rang out over the waters:

"I baptize you with water for repentance, but He who is coming after me is mightier than I... He will baptize you with the Holy Spirit and with fire."

The wind picked up, carrying whispers of a time yet to come.

Adrian could almost feel the heat of the flames, though no fire was visible. This was not the consuming fire of destruction—this was the refining fire of transformation.

And then he saw it.

A room filled with men and women, waiting, praying. A sound like rushing wind filled the air, and suddenly, flames—tongues of fire—descended upon them.

Pentecost.

Adrian's hands trembled as he read. This fire was not meant to destroy, but to empower. It was the fire of the Spirit, the very breath of the Author Himself.

The Call To The Fire

His thoughts spun wildly.

The fire was coming.

Not just in judgment, but in power.

It was the final piece of the story—the purification, the fulfillment, the completion of all things. The Spirit and fire had already been given, yet the greatest fire was still to come.

Adrian flipped the page, his heart pounding.

"The day of the Lord will come as a thief in the night. The heavens will pass away with a great noise, and the elements will melt with fervent heat. But we, according to His promise, look for new heavens and a new earth, in which righteousness dwells."

His throat was dry. He could see it now. The fire was not an end.

It was a beginning.

A refining.

A rebirth.

The book seemed to pulse in his hands, alive with the urgency of its message.

And then he saw the final words of the chapter:

"You have seen the water. You have known the blood. But will you step into the fire?"

Adrian slammed the book shut, his breath ragged.

The choice was before him.

The question was no longer *what* the story was about.

It was whether he would step into it.

A Moment Of Decision

The next morning, Adrian found himself at the library doors before they even opened.

The librarian met him with that same knowing smile. "I take it the book is still speaking?"

Adrian nodded, gripping the book tighter. "It's not just a book."

"No," the librarian agreed. "It's an invitation."

Adrian hesitated. "What does the fire mean for me?"

The librarian studied him for a long moment. "The fire is the final purification, Adrian. The Spirit refines those who are willing, but the world itself will also be cleansed. The question is… will you stand before it as one who has been purified, or one who will be consumed?"

Adrian swallowed hard. The answer should have terrified him.

But for the first time, it didn't.

Because the Author had not abandoned him.

The flames were coming. But perhaps, just perhaps, they were not meant to destroy him.

They were meant to make him new.

CHAPTER 5: THE TRUMPET'S CALL

T he streets were silent as Adrian walked home, the weight of the book heavier than ever. The fire had been revealed— not just a judgment, but a transformation. A refining.

And yet, he could not shake the feeling that something was still missing.

The water had cleansed.
The blood had redeemed.
The fire would purify.

But then what?

Adrian knew the book held the answer. He just wasn't sure he was ready for it.

The Sound That Shakes The Earth

His hands trembled as he opened the book once more, the golden script flickering in the candlelight. The words stretched across the page, drawing him in.

"Then the heavens will tremble, and the trumpet will sound."

A chill ran down his spine.

"The dead in Christ will rise first, and we who are alive and remain shall be caught up to meet Him in the air."

The words were familiar—he had heard them before, whispered in the quiet halls of churches and written in letters from long ago.

But now, they felt alive.

Adrian turned the page, and suddenly, the world around him shifted.

He was no longer in his small room.

He was standing in the middle of a vast plain, the sky dark with an eerie stillness. The air itself seemed to be holding its breath.

And then—

A sound.

It was unlike anything Adrian had ever heard. A blast that shook the heavens, splitting the sky in two. A trumpet, clear and piercing, yet filled with a kind of unearthly melody.

The ground trembled beneath his feet.

The heavens lit up.

And then, movement.

Tombs breaking open. People rising. A light so brilliant that Adrian had to shield his eyes.

It was happening.

The resurrection.

The moment the book had been leading to all along.

The Gathering Of The Saints

Adrian could see them—figures rising from the dust, bodies no longer frail or broken but glowing with a brilliance he could scarcely comprehend. He turned and saw others still standing on the earth, eyes wide with astonishment.

And then they, too, were caught up.

Drawn upward, toward the light.

Adrian's chest tightened. The words of the book echoed in his mind.

"Behold, I tell you a mystery: We shall not all sleep, but we shall all be changed, in a moment, in the twinkling of an eye."

He could feel the truth of it reverberating in his bones. This was no fairy tale. No myth.

This was the promise.

This was the fulfillment of everything.

And yet...

His feet were still on the ground.

He was not rising.

The realization hit him like a blow to the chest.

The Last Call

Panic surged through him. He tried to move, to run toward the light, but his feet were planted firmly in the dust.

Why?

His hands gripped the book tightly, his knuckles white. The answer was there, hidden in the pages.

And then he saw it:

"Watch therefore, for you do not know the hour your Lord is coming."

The words burned into his mind.

"Not everyone who says to Me, 'Lord, Lord,' shall enter the Kingdom."

Adrian's breath came in ragged gasps.

He had seen the water. He had accepted the blood. He had stood before the fire.

But had he truly surrendered?

Had he truly given his life to the Author?

He turned the page with shaking hands.

"The Spirit and the Bride say, 'Come!' Let him who hears say,

'Come!'"

It was not too late.

The invitation was still open.

But for how much longer?

The Moment Of Decision

The vision faded, and Adrian was back in his room, the book clutched to his chest.

His heart was pounding, his breath uneven.

The trumpet had not yet sounded. The sky had not yet split open.

But it would.

And when it did, there would be no second chances.

He pushed himself to his feet, his resolve hardening. He had spent too long asking questions, too long searching for answers without stepping forward in faith.

The invitation had been given.

And he was ready to answer it.

A Final Warning

The next morning, Adrian made his way back to the library one last time.

The librarian was waiting, as if he had known Adrian would return.

"I understand now," Adrian said, his voice steady. "The story isn't just about the past. It's about the future."

The librarian nodded. "Yes. And your place in it."

Adrian took a deep breath. "The trumpet hasn't sounded yet. But when it does… I want to be ready."

A slow smile spread across the librarian's face. "Then let the Author write your next chapter."

Adrian looked down at the book one last time.

Then, with newfound resolve, he closed it.

The story wasn't over.

It was just beginning.

CHAPTER 6: THE VEIL AND THE THRONE

Adrian sat at his desk, staring at the closed book. His heart still thundered from the vision of the trumpet's call. The fire had been revealing, the blood had been cleansing, the water had been purifying.

But now, he knew there was something beyond it all.

Something greater.

Something final.

Slowly, he reached for the book, hesitating for only a moment before opening it once more.

The words on the page shimmered.

"Come up here, and I will show you what must take place."

A sharp gasp escaped his lips as the world around him shifted.

The room, the desk, the candlelight—they all dissolved.

And Adrian was standing before a veil.

Beyond The Veil

It towered before him, stretching infinitely in every direction. A shimmering barrier of light and shadow, of time and eternity.

The air hummed with power.

Adrian stepped forward, drawn by something unseen.

And then, with a whisper like a breath from another world, the veil **parted**.

His breath caught in his throat.

On the other side, an expanse of brilliance awaited—a throne room unlike anything he could have imagined.

The Throne Of The Ancient One

Adrian fell to his knees.

Before him was the Throne.

The One who sat upon it shone with an unbearable light, clothed in fire and majesty, yet veiled in a presence so overwhelming that Adrian could not lift his gaze.

Lightning flashed around the Throne, illuminating what stood before it.

Twenty-four elders cast their crowns upon the glass-like sea. Multitudes upon multitudes stood before the King, their voices blending into a song that shook the heavens.

"Holy, holy, holy, is the Lord God Almighty, who was, and is, and is to come!"

Adrian's heart pounded as his gaze was drawn to something else.

At the center of it all—before the Throne, between the elders— stood the **Lamb**.

Slain, yet alive.

Blood-marked, yet radiant.

He knew in an instant who He was.

This was the One the book had spoken of. The One who had been promised. The One who had given His life.

And now—

The One who was returning.

Adrian's vision blurred as the song of the multitudes thundered around him.

"Worthy is the Lamb who was slain, to receive power and riches and wisdom, and strength and honor and glory and blessing!"

Every soul, every being, every voice cried out in worship.

And then—

A silence fell.

The One on the Throne rose.

A scroll was in His hand.

Sealed.

Seven times over.

Adrian's breath hitched. He knew what this was. The book had spoken of it.

The scroll—the final decree. The unveiling of all that was to come.

And yet...

No one could open it.

A sorrow so deep it seemed to shake the heavens spread across the assembly.

"Who is worthy?" a voice called.

"Who is worthy to break the seals and open the scroll?"

Silence.

A silence so vast, so infinite, that it swallowed every song, every breath, every hope.

Adrian's chest tightened. If no one could open it...

Then the story could not continue.

The judgment, the restoration, the promise—it would remain sealed forever.

He clenched his fists, his spirit crying out with the same longing that filled the heavens.

But then—

A movement.

A voice.

"Do not weep."

A hand pointed toward the center of the Throne room.

"Behold! The Lion of the tribe of Judah, the Root of David, has triumphed! He is worthy to open the scroll!"

Adrian turned—

And there He was.

The **Lamb** stepped forward.

The fire in His eyes burned with holiness and mercy.

He reached out—

And **took the scroll from the hand of the One seated on the Throne**.

The heavens **erupted**.

The song began again, shaking the very foundations of existence.

"To Him who sits on the throne and to the Lamb be praise and honor and glory and power, forever and ever!"

The time had come.

The seals would be broken.

The final chapter would begin.

The Unfolding Of The End

Adrian gasped as he was suddenly pulled back—ripped from the vision and thrust into the stillness of his room.

His chest heaved. His hands trembled.

The book lay open before him, the final words of the vision glowing faintly.

"The time is near. He who is coming will not delay."

Adrian wiped a shaking hand across his face. He had seen it.

The Throne.

The Lamb.

The scroll.

The seals would soon be broken.

The last days were not far off.

And when they came, everything—**everything**—would change.

Adrian leaned back in his chair, staring up at the ceiling.

He was no longer just a reader of the story.

He was a part of it.

And now, there was no turning back.

CHAPTER 7: THE BREAKING OF THE SEALS

Adrian could barely move. The vision of the Throne, the Lamb, and the scroll still burned within his mind. He had seen it—the heavens trembling, the multitudes crying out in worship, the fire in the eyes of the One who held the sealed decree.

But now, something deeper stirred in him.

The seals would be broken.

The final chapter of the story was about to unfold.

With a deep breath, Adrian reached for the book again. His fingers trembled as he turned the page.

And then—

The words **pulled him in**.

The First Seal: The White Horse

A great silence filled the heavens.

Adrian found himself standing once more in the Throne Room, his heart hammering. The Lamb held the scroll, His fingers resting upon the first seal.

And then—

He broke it.

A voice thundered through the heavens:

"Come!"

Adrian turned toward the sound, and his breath caught in his throat.

A **white horse** emerged from the light, its rider cloaked in brilliance. A golden crown rested on his brow, and in his hand, he held a bow.

The rider raised his weapon, and Adrian could feel it—**the beginning of conquest**.

"He went out conquering and to conquer."

Adrian clenched his fists. This was no ordinary ruler. This was the rise of deception—the one who would come in the name of peace, yet bring war.

The world would believe in his promise.

But they would not see the darkness hidden beneath his crown.

The Second Seal: The Red Horse

The Lamb broke the second seal.

Again, a voice cried out:

"Come!"

A second horse charged forward—**red as blood**.

Its rider carried a great sword, and as he rode, Adrian saw the world below erupt into chaos.

Nations warring. Cities burning. Brother turning against brother.

"Peace was taken from the earth, and men slayed one another."

Adrian's stomach twisted. The first rider had deceived the nations with false peace. But this one—this one brought **war**.

And war would not stop until the world was consumed by its fury.

The Third Seal: The Black Horse

The third seal was broken.

A third voice called:

"Come!"

A black horse emerged, its rider holding scales in his hand.

Adrian felt a weight press upon him as he heard the decree:

"A measure of wheat for a denarius, and three measures of barley for a denarius. But do not harm the oil and the wine."

Famine.

The world would starve.

Not just in hunger, but in desperation. The powerful would hoard what remained, while the poor suffered beyond imagining.

Adrian swallowed hard. The seals were unfolding **exactly as the book had foretold**.

And yet, there was more.

The Fourth Seal: The Pale Horse

The fourth seal was broken.

The final voice called:

"Come!"

A **pale horse** thundered forth, its rider draped in shadows. Adrian knew his name before it was spoken.

Death.

And behind him, following closely—

Hades.

Adrian's knees nearly gave out.

"Power was given to them over a fourth of the earth, to kill with

sword, with hunger, with death, and by the beasts of the earth."

He saw it all unfold—plagues sweeping across nations, the earth itself groaning as death claimed its due.

The first four seals had brought deception, war, famine, and death.

And the world had **no idea what was coming next**.

The Fifth Seal: The Cry Of The Martyrs

The Lamb broke the **fifth seal**.

Adrian turned, expecting another rider.

But instead, he saw **souls beneath the altar**.

They were crying out—voices lifted to heaven in sorrow and longing.

"How long, O Lord, holy and true, until You judge and avenge our blood?"

They were those who had died for the truth.

Those who had refused the deception.

Adrian felt tears burn his eyes as he watched white robes being given to them.

"Rest a little while longer, until the number of your fellow servants is completed."

The suffering was not yet over.

But justice **was coming**.

The Sixth Seal: The Shaking Of The Earth

The Lamb broke the **sixth seal**.

And the heavens **split open**.

Adrian gasped as the **sun turned black** and the **moon became as blood**.

The very earth beneath him **trembled**.

"The stars fell from the sky, and the heavens rolled up like a scroll."

Mountains crumbled. Kings and rulers **fled in terror**, crying out for the rocks to cover them.

"Hide us from the face of Him who sits on the Throne, and from the wrath of the Lamb!"

Adrian's entire body trembled.

The world had ignored the warning signs.

But now—

Now, they knew.

Now, **they saw Him**.

And terror consumed them.

A Pause Before The Seventh Seal

Adrian felt himself **pulled back**, the vision fading.

He gasped, hands gripping the edges of the book. His entire body was drenched in sweat.

The seals—

They had been revealed.

But there was one more.

His fingers hovered over the next page.

He already knew.

The **seventh seal** would change **everything**.

And once it was broken, there would be no more delay.

His heart pounded.

The story wasn't over.

The final judgment was still ahead.

But one thing was certain—

The end had begun.

CHAPTER 8: THE SEVENTH SEAL AND THE SILENCE

Adrian's breath came in shallow gasps. The weight of the vision pressed upon him, the breaking of the seals still fresh in his mind.

The White Horse of deception.

The Red Horse of war.

The Black Horse of famine.

The Pale Horse of death.

The cries of the martyrs.

The shaking of the heavens.

Six seals had been broken.

Only one remained.

Adrian's fingers trembled as he turned the page, feeling the pull of something inevitable. The golden script shimmered, drawing him into the final seal.

And then—

Silence.

The Silence In Heaven

Adrian found himself once again standing before the Throne.

The hosts of heaven surrounded him—the elders, the multitudes, the living creatures who had worshiped without ceasing.

But now—

No one spoke.

No one moved.

The heavens were silent.

For **half an hour**, the Throne Room stood still, as if **all of creation held its breath**.

Adrian could hear nothing but the pounding of his own heartbeat.

Then he saw it.

Before the Throne, **seven angels stood in formation**. Each held a trumpet, their faces set with an expression that Adrian could not quite understand.

Anticipation.

Sorrow.

Judgment.

One by one, they lifted their trumpets.

And the silence was broken.

The Prayers Of The Saints

A new figure emerged before the Throne—an angel clothed in light, carrying a golden censer filled with **incense and fire from the altar**.

Adrian recognized it immediately.

"The prayers of the saints."

The angel lifted the censer high, and the fragrance of the prayers filled the heavens, rising before the presence of God.

Adrian's heart ached. He could feel the weight of them—every whispered petition, every tearful cry, every plea for justice that had gone unanswered for generations.

41

And then—

The angel took the censer and **cast it upon the earth**.

Thunder roared.

Lightning slashed across the sky.

The ground trembled with a force so great that Adrian staggered back, barely able to keep his footing.

He knew what it meant.

The time of waiting was over.

The final judgments had begun.

The First Trumpet: Fire And Blood

The first angel **raised his trumpet**—

And blew.

Immediately, Adrian saw fire rain down from the sky.

"Hail and fire, mingled with blood, were thrown to the earth."

Forests erupted in flame. Fields blackened into ash. Cities were swallowed by an inferno that showed no mercy.

"A third of the trees were burned up, and all the green grass was scorched."

Adrian's breath hitched.

This was no ordinary fire.

This was the beginning of **the great shaking**.

The Second Trumpet: The Mountain Of Fire

The **second angel** lifted his trumpet—

And blew.

A massive form hurtled from the heavens—**a great mountain, burning with fire**.

It struck the sea with a force that sent waves crashing into the land, swallowing ships and cities alike.

"A third of the sea became blood, and a third of all living creatures in it perished."

Adrian's hands clenched into fists. The ocean churned red, bodies drifting lifelessly in the waves.

The **world's waters were dying**.

And the world had barely begun to feel the weight of what was coming.

The Third Trumpet: The Falling Star

The **third angel** raised his trumpet—

And blew.

A star **blazed across the heavens**, streaking toward the earth like a dying ember.

"And the name of the star was Wormwood."

It struck the rivers and lakes, poisoning the fresh waters.

"A third of the waters became bitter, and many men died from the water, because it was made poisonous."

Adrian saw people collapse, their bodies wracked with agony.

What was once life-giving had turned into death.

He clenched his jaw.

The world was being undone.

One seal.

One trumpet.

One judgment at a time.

The Fourth Trumpet: Darkness Falls

The **fourth angel** lifted his trumpet—

And blew.

The sky itself seemed to shudder.

"A third of the sun was struck, a third of the moon, and a third of the stars."

Adrian watched in horror as darkness **fell upon the world**.

Daylight dimmed. The night lost its stars.

The earth was plunged into a shadow that no flame could dispel.

And then—

The silence returned.

Not the silence of reverence.

But the silence **before a storm**.

Adrian looked up, his pulse hammering.

And that's when he saw it.

A shadow sweeping across the sky, its wings vast and terrible.

A voice rang out—

A single word, carried on the wind like an omen.

"Woe… woe… woe to the inhabitants of the earth."

Adrian's blood ran cold.

The worst was still to come.

The Final Warning

The vision faded, and Adrian was back in his room, the book **glowing** in his lap.

His body trembled.

His spirit ached.

The seventh seal had been broken.

The first four trumpets had sounded.

And yet—

He knew that something **even greater** was approaching.

Something **no one** was ready for.

Adrian wiped a shaking hand across his face.

He had seen the Lamb. He had stood before the Throne.

And now, he had witnessed the **beginning of the end**.

The story was no longer distant.

It was happening.

And the question was no longer *if* he believed.

It was whether he would be **ready**.

CHAPTER 9: THE ABYSS OPENS

A drian's hands trembled as he turned the page. The visions of the first four trumpets still burned in his mind—fire and blood, poisoned waters, choking darkness—but he knew something even greater lay ahead.

The voice of warning still echoed:

"Woe, woe, woe to the inhabitants of the earth!"

A shiver ran down his spine. The final three trumpets would be worse than anything he had yet seen.

And the world was not ready.

The Fifth Trumpet: The Abyss Unleashed

Adrian was pulled back into the vision.

The sky churned with an unnatural darkness, as if the very heavens had been **torn open**.

The **fifth angel** lifted his trumpet—

And blew.

A great star **fell from heaven**.

But unlike Wormwood, this was no ordinary falling body.

This star **had a key**.

Adrian's heart pounded as the star approached a massive **gate**

—one so ancient and terrible that even the ground beneath it seemed to recoil.

Then, with a single movement, the star **unlocked the Abyss**.

A blast of **smoke and fire** erupted from the depths, blotting out what little light remained in the sky. Adrian coughed, his lungs burning as the air filled with a suffocating presence.

And then, they came.

Creatures—neither human nor beast—rose from the chasm.

They swarmed like locusts, their wings creating a thunderous, deafening sound. Their bodies were armored, their faces twisted into nightmarish forms that seemed both familiar and wholly unnatural.

And at their head—

A king.

"They had as king over them the angel of the bottomless pit, whose name in Hebrew is Abaddon, and in Greek, Apollyon."

Adrian staggered backward.

The **Destroyer had risen**.

The creatures did not kill.

No—**they tormented**.

Adrian watched in horror as they descended upon those left on the earth. Their victims screamed, clutching their heads in agony. They longed for death, but it would not come.

"In those days men will seek death and will not find it. They will desire to die, but death will flee from them."

Adrian clenched his fists. He had seen war, famine, and plagues.

But **this**—

This was demonic.

And it was only the beginning.

The Sixth Trumpet: The Four Angels Released

The **sixth angel** raised his trumpet—

And blew.

Immediately, a voice came from the altar before the Throne:

"Release the four angels who are bound at the great river Euphrates."

Adrian turned, his breath catching.

He saw them.

Bound in chains.

Waiting.

Four figures, their presence like shadows stretching across the horizon. They had been imprisoned for **millennia**, held back for **this very moment**.

Now, their restraints were gone.

And Adrian felt the shift in the fabric of the world.

These were not mere angels.

These were **warriors of destruction**.

They mounted their horses—terrible, monstrous creatures with heads like lions and breath like fire.

And as they rode—

"A third of mankind was killed."

Adrian's stomach twisted. Cities fell. The land trembled beneath the weight of their charge. The sky burned with the wrath they unleashed.

It was war.

It was **slaughter**.

It was **unstoppable**.

And yet—

Even in the face of such devastation, Adrian saw something even more terrifying.

"But the rest of mankind did not repent of their works."

His heart ached.

The world had seen the fire.

They had endured the darkness.

They had suffered through war and plague.

And **still**, they refused to turn to the One who could save them.

Tears blurred his vision.

Why?

Why would they not turn?

Why would they **not see**?

Adrian fell to his knees, fists pressed against the ground.

The answer came like a whisper through the smoke.

Because **their hearts were hardened**.

Because **they had chosen this path**.

Because **they had rejected the truth**.

And now—

The final trumpet was near.

The Final Pause: A Mighty Angel And A Little Scroll

The vision shifted.

Adrian found himself standing before a **mighty angel**, whose face burned like the sun and whose feet blazed like pillars of fire.

In his hand—

A **small scroll**, open and waiting.

The angel placed one foot on the sea and one foot on the land, lifting his hand toward heaven.

And then, he **swore an oath**.

"There shall be no more delay."

The words thundered through Adrian's soul.

No more delay.

No more waiting.

The final moment was coming.

And nothing could stop it.

The angel handed Adrian the little scroll.

"Take and eat it."

Adrian hesitated before lifting the scroll to his lips.

The moment it touched his tongue, a strange sensation overtook him—

Sweet.

Then—

Bitter.

The truth of what was coming **burned** within him.

The promise of the kingdom was near.

But so was the **final judgment**.

Adrian's vision blurred as the weight of it all pressed upon him.

And then—

He was back in his room.

The book lay open before him, the golden script still glowing faintly.

The world was on the edge of eternity.

And there was no more time to wait.

Adrian exhaled shakily.

He had seen the fire.

He had seen the blood.

He had seen the heavens tremble.

But now, he had seen the **Abyss itself open**.

And he knew—

The story was nearly complete.

The seventh trumpet was about to sound.

And when it did, the world would never be the same again.

CHAPTER 10: THE SEVENTH TRUMPET AND THE UNVEILING OF THE KINGDOM

Adrian sat in silence, his breath unsteady. The visions of the previous trumpets still burned in his mind— the abyss opening, demonic torment, the four angels of destruction, the hardened hearts of mankind.

And yet, he could feel something shifting.

The story was nearing its climax.

The book in his hands seemed to pulse with anticipation, the golden script glowing with a quiet intensity.

Adrian turned the page.

And the final trumpet sounded.

The Seventh Trumpet: The Kingdom Declared

The **seventh angel** raised his trumpet—

And blew.

Adrian braced himself, expecting another catastrophe, another plague, another war.

But instead—

The heavens **erupted in worship**.

"The kingdoms of this world have become the Kingdom of our Lord and of His Christ, and He shall reign forever and ever!"

Adrian gasped.

It was **not destruction**.

It was **victory**.

The voices of multitudes filled the air, their praise shaking the very foundations of creation. He looked up and saw **the Throne** once again, shining with a brilliance that outshone even the fire and storm surrounding it.

The **elders fell on their faces**, casting their crowns before the King.

"We give You thanks, O Lord God Almighty, the One who is and who was and who is to come, because You have taken Your great power and have reigned!"

Adrian's chest tightened.

The story was reaching its fulfillment.

The King was **taking His throne**.

And yet—

Something else was still to come.

The Temple In Heaven Opened

Adrian's gaze was drawn to a **great light**.

The **Temple in heaven** stood before him, its doors suddenly thrown wide open.

And within—

The **Ark of the Covenant** was revealed.

Lightning flashed.

Thunder roared.

The earth trembled beneath the weight of its unveiling.

Adrian knew what this meant.

God's presence—His **glory**—was now fully revealed.

No more veils.

No more hidden mysteries.

The **heavenly and the earthly realms** were colliding.

The **Kingdom had come**.

And judgment would follow.

The Final Conflict Begins

The scene shifted.

Adrian saw a **woman clothed with the sun**, standing in the heavens, a **crown of twelve stars** upon her head.

Beneath her feet—**the moon**.

Her cry echoed through the heavens as she travailed in labor, ready to give birth.

Then—

A **great red dragon** emerged from the darkness, its seven heads rearing up in defiance. Its tail swept across the heavens, tearing down a third of the stars.

Adrian's hands clenched.

This was the battle the book had been leading to all along.

The **Dragon** was rising.

And the war for the world had begun.

War In Heaven

A deafening **roar** split the sky.

Adrian turned and saw **Michael**, the great archangel, **leading the**

armies of heaven.

Their swords flashed like lightning as they clashed with the Dragon and his forces. The heavens **shook** with the force of their battle.

Adrian's heart pounded.

Then, with a final, thunderous **blow**, the Dragon was **cast down** —hurled from the heavens, falling like a dying star.

A voice rang out:

"Woe to the inhabitants of the earth, for the devil has come down to you, having great wrath, because he knows that his time is short!"

Adrian's stomach twisted.

The **Kingdom had been declared**.

But the **final battle was beginning**.

The Mark Of The Beast

The vision shifted again.

Adrian saw a **beast rise from the sea**, its body covered in **scars and crowns**, its voice filled with **blasphemy**.

The world **worshiped it**.

And then—

Another beast emerged from the earth, deceiving the people with **signs and wonders**.

"He causes all, both small and great, rich and poor, free and slave, to receive a mark on their right hand or on their foreheads."

Adrian felt his throat tighten.

"No one may buy or sell except the one who has the mark."

He watched as the world was divided—**those who bore the mark of the Beast, and those who refused**.

The deception was complete.

The war had begun.

And now—

The King would return.

The Harvest Of The Earth

The sky **split open**.

Adrian lifted his eyes—

And saw **One seated on a white cloud**.

A **crown of gold** rested on His head.

And in His hand—

A **sickle**.

A voice cried out:

"Thrust in Your sickle and reap, for the harvest of the earth is ripe!"

The **final gathering** had begun.

Adrian watched as **the righteous were gathered first**, their souls taken into the presence of the King.

Then, another sickle appeared—

And this time, it was **for judgment**.

The **winepress of God's wrath** was trampled.

The earth **was cleansed**.

The war **was over**.

And the **King was coming**.

The Rider On The White Horse

Adrian barely had time to process what he had seen before the heavens **erupted** again.

This time, it was not destruction.

It was **glory**.

He looked up—

And saw **Him**.

The **Faithful and True One**.

The **Rider on the White Horse**.

His eyes **blazed like fire**.

A robe **dipped in blood** billowed behind Him.

And upon His thigh was written:

"King of Kings and Lord of Lords."

Adrian could hardly breathe.

This was it.

This was **the moment creation had been waiting for**.

The **King was coming to reign**.

The **war was over**.

The **story was complete**.

And **the Kingdom had come**.

A New Beginning

The vision faded.

Adrian gasped, his body trembling.

The book lay open in his hands, **the final words glowing with light**.

"Behold, I am coming quickly. My reward is with Me, to give to each one according to his work."

Adrian exhaled shakily.

The Kingdom was no longer a distant promise.

It was a **reality**.

And soon, the **world would see it**.

He closed the book, his heart steady.

The next chapter wasn't his to write.

It was the **King's**.

And when He came—

Everything would be made new.

CHAPTER 11: A NEW HEAVEN AND A NEW EARTH

Adrian sat in stunned silence, the weight of the visions pressing upon him like an ocean tide. He had seen the Lamb take His throne, the final battle waged, and the war for the earth brought to its climactic end.

And yet—

Something told him the story wasn't over.

Not yet.

He turned the final pages of the book, his breath steady but expectant.

And suddenly—

Everything changed.

The Thousand Years

The battlefield was **silent**.

Adrian watched as the **King of Kings** stood victorious, His robe still stained with the blood of His enemies. Behind Him, the **armies of heaven** stood in solemn triumph.

And before Him—

The **Dragon** lay in chains.

"Then I saw an angel coming down from heaven, having the key to

the bottomless pit and a great chain in his hand."

Adrian's heart pounded.

The same abyss that had once unleashed **torment upon the earth** was now the Dragon's **prison**.

The angel raised his voice:

"He laid hold of the dragon, that serpent of old, who is the devil and Satan, and bound him for a thousand years."

Adrian watched as **the abyss yawned open** once more, swallowing the adversary in a darkness so absolute it seemed to stretch into eternity.

The door **slammed shut**.

Sealed.

The deceiver was **locked away**.

And peace—true peace—descended upon the earth.

The Millennial Kingdom

Adrian turned, his breath catching at what he saw.

The world was **restored**.

Cities **gleamed** with light, free from corruption. The air was clean, the rivers flowed with purity, the very fabric of creation seemed **reborn**.

And at the center of it all—

Jerusalem.

The **City of the King**.

He saw the **thrones of the righteous**, those who had endured to the end, those who had given their lives for the Lamb.

They ruled **with Him**.

And the nations **worshiped**.

For a thousand years, **there was no war, no death, no deception.**

Just **peace**.

Just **righteousness**.

Just **the reign of the King**.

Adrian's soul ached with a longing he had never known.

This was how the world was always **meant to be**.

The Final Rebellion

But then—

A shadow crept upon the horizon.

Adrian turned and saw **the abyss open one last time**.

The Dragon **rose again**, his fury unquenched, his deception still festering.

"When the thousand years have expired, Satan will be released from his prison and will go out to deceive the nations."

Adrian gritted his teeth.

Even after a thousand years of **perfect peace**, there were **still** those who would choose rebellion.

Still those who would believe **the lie**.

Nations gathered once more, armies marching against the **Holy City**, foolishly believing they could **overthrow the Throne of God**.

And then—

Fire fell from heaven.

It was over in an instant.

"The devil, who deceived them, was cast into the lake of fire and brimstone, where the beast and the false prophet are. And they will be tormented day and night forever and ever."

Adrian exhaled, his body trembling.

The deceiver was **gone**.

Forever.

And now—

The final judgment would begin.

The Great White Throne

Adrian turned the page.

And suddenly—

He was standing before **the Throne** once more.

But this time, it was not surrounded by worship.

It was surrounded by **souls**.

Countless **souls**.

"Then I saw a great white throne and Him who sat on it, from whose face the earth and the heavens fled away."

Adrian's throat tightened.

The **books were opened**.

And every deed, every word, every secret was **laid bare**.

No more deception.

No more excuses.

"And anyone not found written in the Book of Life was cast into the lake of fire."

Tears burned Adrian's eyes.

This was the final moment.

The final separation.

And then—

The old world was **gone**.

The sky.

The earth.

Everything **vanished**.

And a new **beginning** was about to unfold.

A New Heaven And A New Earth

Adrian turned the last page.

And what he saw took his breath away.

The world was **new**.

Not just **restored—remade**.

"Now I saw a new heaven and a new earth, for the first heaven and the first earth had passed away."

The sky stretched endless and clear.

The land was untouched by corruption.

The rivers shone like **crystal**, flowing from the very Throne of God.

And descending from above—

A city.

Not like any city Adrian had ever seen.

This was **the Holy City, the New Jerusalem**.

It shone with the **glory of God**, its foundations made of **precious stones**, its gates of **pure pearl**, its streets **like transparent gold**.

And at the center—

The **Lamb**.

"Behold, the tabernacle of God is with men, and He will dwell with them. They shall be His people, and God Himself will be with them and be their God."

Adrian fell to his knees.

There was **no more death**.

No more pain.

No more sorrow.

No more separation.

"Behold, I make all things new."

The Invitation

The vision began to fade.

Adrian felt himself being pulled back, the golden script of the book **glowing brighter than ever**.

He looked at the final words, his heart pounding.

"The Spirit and the Bride say, 'Come!' And let him who hears say, 'Come!' And let him who thirsts come. Whoever desires, let him take the water of life freely."

Adrian swallowed hard.

The story was finished.

The Kingdom had come.

Eternity had begun.

And the invitation was still open.

For **anyone**.

For **everyone**.

For **him**.

The Last Amen

Adrian closed the book.

Tears streaked his face, but he was **smiling**.

Because he knew—

This wasn't the end.

This was the **beginning**.

He stood, lifting his face to the sky, the final words still ringing in his soul.

"Surely I am coming quickly."

And Adrian whispered the only response possible.

"Even so, come, Lord Jesus."

Amen.

FURTHER STUDY: UNDERSTANDING THE 7,000-YEAR PLAN AND THE PRE-TRIBULATION RAPTURE

1. The 7,000-Year Prophetic Timeline

One of the central themes of *7000 Years* is the belief that **God has structured human history into a 7,000-year plan**, mirroring the **seven days of creation** (Genesis 1-2). The Bible gives clues that a **day is as a thousand years to the Lord** (2 Peter 3:8), suggesting that history follows this pattern:

The Six Days Of Work (6,000 Years Of Human History)

- **First 2,000 Years (The Age of the Patriarchs - Water & Judgment)**
    - From **Adam to Noah's Flood** (~4,000 BC - ~2,000 BC).
    - Marked by increasing wickedness, leading to the judgment of the flood.

- *Foreshadowing: Water cleansed the world, just as baptism cleanses believers.*

- **Second 2,000 Years (The Age of Israel - Blood & Redemption)**
  - From **Abraham to Christ's Crucifixion** (~2,000 BC - ~33 AD).
  - Marked by the covenant with Israel and the sacrifices under the Law.
  - *Foreshadowing: The blood of lambs covered sins until the ultimate sacrifice of Christ.*

- **Final 2,000 Years (The Church Age - Spirit & Grace)**
  - From **Christ's resurrection to today (~33 AD - present).**
  - Marked by the spread of the Gospel and the indwelling of the Holy Spirit.
  - *Foreshadowing: The Spirit of God works in believers, preparing them for Christ's return.*

The Seventh Day: 1,000 Years Of Rest (The Millennial Kingdom)

- **The last 1,000 years (Millennial Reign of Christ - The Sabbath Rest)**
  - Christ **rules the earth for 1,000 years** (Revelation 20:4).
  - Satan is bound, peace is restored, and righteousness fills the earth.
  - *Foreshadowing: Just as God rested on the seventh*

day, the world will experience 1,000 years of divine rest.

2. The Pre-Tribulation Rapture: Why The Church Will Be Taken Before The Tribulation

The **Rapture** is the moment when **Christ removes His Church from the earth before the seven-year Tribulation**. The Bible describes this event as a **"catching up"** (1 Thessalonians 4:16-17).

Biblical Evidence For The Pre-Tribulation Rapture

- **Jesus' Promise to Keep Believers from Wrath**
    - *"Because you have kept My command to persevere, I also will keep you from the hour of trial which shall come upon the whole world."* (Revelation 3:10)
- **The Church is Not Mentioned in Tribulation Passages**
    - After **Revelation 3**, the Church **is not mentioned** during the events of the Tribulation (Revelation 6-19).
    - Instead, **Israel and the nations** become the focus, indicating the Church is gone.
- **The Rapture is Different from the Second Coming**
    - The **Rapture**: Christ **comes for His Bride** and meets believers **in the air** (1 Thessalonians 4:16-17).
    - The **Second Coming**: Christ **returns with His Bride** to the earth to reign (Revelation 19:11-16).

- **The Days of Noah and Lot**
  - Jesus compared the end times to the days of **Noah and Lot** (Luke 17:26-30).
  - In both cases, **God removed the righteous before judgment fell**—Noah in the ark and Lot from Sodom.
  - The **Rapture follows this pattern**—the Church is removed before Tribulation begins.

3. The Tribulation: The Seven-Year Judgment After The Rapture

Once the Church is removed, **God's judgment begins on the unbelieving world**. This **seven-year period** is known as **Daniel's 70th Week** (Daniel 9:27) and is marked by:

The Key Events of the Tribulation

- **The Antichrist Confirms a Peace Treaty (Daniel 9:27).**
- **The Seals, Trumpets, and Bowls of Wrath (Revelation 6-19).**
- **The Rise of the One-World Government and Mark of the Beast (Revelation 13).**
- **The Persecution of Tribulation Saints (Matthew 24:21).**
- **The Second Coming of Christ and Armageddon (Revelation 19:11-21).**

4. The Second Coming Of Christ And The Millennial Kingdom

At the end of the Tribulation, Jesus Christ **returns physically to the earth** and defeats the Antichrist at **Armageddon** (Revelation 19:11-21).

Key Events of the Second Coming & Millennium

- **Satan is bound for 1,000 years (Revelation 20:1-3).**
- **Christ reigns from Jerusalem (Revelation 20:4-6).**
- **The earth is restored, and righteousness fills the world (Isaiah 11:6-9).**

5. The Final Judgment And The New Heaven & Earth

After the **1,000-year reign**, Satan is released for one final rebellion but is quickly defeated. Then comes the **Great White Throne Judgment**.

- **Revelation 20:11-15** – *"Then I saw a great white throne and Him who sat on it, from whose face the earth and the heaven fled away."*
- **Anyone not found in the Book of Life is cast into the lake of fire.**
- **God creates a New Heaven and a New Earth (Revelation 21:1-4).**

6. A Call To Readiness: Are You Prepared?

Jesus warned:

"Watch therefore, for you do not know what hour your Lord is coming." (Matthew 24:42)

The Rapture **could happen at any moment**. The question is **not when, but are you ready?**

How to Be Saved

1. **Admit you are a sinner** – *"For all have sinned and fall short of the glory of God."* (Romans 3:23)

2. **Believe that Jesus Christ died for your sins and rose again** – *"But God demonstrates His own love toward us, in that while we were still sinners, Christ died for us."* (Romans 5:8)

3. **Call upon Jesus to save you** – *"Whoever calls on the name of the Lord shall be saved."* (Romans 10:13)

If you have never placed your faith in Jesus Christ, **now is the time**.

Final Thoughts: The Spirit And The Bride Say, 'Come!'

The **last chapter of the Bible** gives **one final invitation**:

"And the Spirit and the Bride say, 'Come!' And let him who hears say, 'Come!' And let him who thirsts come. Whoever desires, let him take the water of life freely." (Revelation 22:17)

The 7,000-year story is almost complete.

Are you ready for the King's return?

APPENDICES

Appendix A: The 7,000-Year
Timeline of Biblical History

Biblical prophecy reveals that God has ordained human history to follow a 7,000-year plan, mirroring the seven days of creation. The Bible suggests that "a day is like a thousand years" to the Lord (2 Peter 3:8), indicating that six thousand years will pass before Christ's 1,000-year reign.

Overview of the 7,000-Year Timeline:

Period	Years	Key Events
1st 2,000 Years (Water – Judgment & Cleansing)	4000 BC – 2000 BC	Creation, Fall of Man, Noah's Flood
2nd 2,000 Years (Blood – Covenant & Redemption)	2000 BC – 33 AD	Abrahamic Covenant, Moses & the Law, Christ's Crucifixion
3rd 2,000 Years (Spirit – The Church Age)	33 AD – Present	The Gospel Preached, The Church Age, Israel's Rebirth (1948)
7th Day – The 1,000-Year Millennial Reign	Future	Christ rules on Earth, Final Judgment, New Heaven & Earth

Appendix B: The Order of End-Time Events

Pre-Tribulation

The Bible clearly lays out a sequence of events leading to the return of Christ and the final judgment. Below is a simplified breakdown of these events:

1. **The Rapture of the Church (Before the Tribulation)**
   - Christ gathers His Church **before judgment begins** (1 Thessalonians 4:16-17).
   - The **restrainer (Holy Spirit in the Church) is removed** (2 Thessalonians 2:6-7).

2. **The Seven-Year Tribulation (Daniel's 70th Week)**
   - The **Antichrist confirms a peace covenant** with Israel (Daniel 9:27).
   - The **Seals, Trumpets, and Bowls** bring **God's judgments** on the earth (Revelation 6-19).
   - The Antichrist **sets up the Mark of the Beast system** (Revelation 13).

3. **The Second Coming of Christ (End of the Tribulation)**
   - Christ **returns with the saints** and defeats the Antichrist at Armageddon (Revelation 19:11-21).
   - Satan is **bound for 1,000 years** (Revelation 20:1-3).

4. **The Millennial Kingdom (1,000-Year Reign of Christ)**
   - Christ **rules the earth from Jerusalem** (Revelation 20:4-6).

5. **The Final Judgment and New Creation**

- Satan is **released, then permanently defeated** (Revelation 20:7-10).

- The **Great White Throne Judgment** for unbelievers (Revelation 20:11-15).

- The creation of the **New Heaven & New Earth** (Revelation 21:1-4).

This confirms that believers in Christ will be taken before the wrath of the Tribulation begins!

Appendix C: The Rapture vs. The Second Coming – What's the Difference?

Many confuse the Rapture and the Second Coming, but the Bible clearly teaches that they are two separate events. Below is a comparison chart:

Event	The Rapture (Before Tribulation)	The Second Coming (After Tribulation)
Who is taken?	The **Church (believers) are taken** to heaven	The **wicked are removed**, believers remain
Who remains?	The **unsaved remain** on earth	Believers enter Christ's Kingdom
Where does Jesus appear?	**In the air** (1 Thess. 4:16-17)	**On Earth – Mount of Olives** (Zech. 14:4)
Purpose?	To **gather the Church** before judgment	To **judge the nations & establish His reign**
Biblical Passages	1 Thessalonians 4:16-17, 1 Corinthians 15:51-52	Revelation 19:11-16, Zechariah 14:3-4

This confirms that the Church is NOT destined for wrath but will be taken before the final judgment begins!

*Appendix D: The Seals, Trumpets, and
Bowls – God's Judgment in Revelation*

The Book of Revelation describes three series of judgments that occur during the Tribulation. Below is a breakdown of each set of judgments:

The Seven Seals (Revelation 6)

1. **The White Horse** – The Antichrist brings a false peace.
2. **The Red Horse** – War spreads across the earth.
3. **The Black Horse** – Famine devastates nations.
4. **The Pale Horse** – Death claims a quarter of humanity.
5. **The Cry of the Martyrs** – Believers are slain for their faith.
6. **The Great Earthquake** – Cosmic disturbances shake the world.
7. **The Silence in Heaven** – The final judgments prepare to be released.

The Seven Trumpets (Revelation 8-11)

1. **Hail & Fire Mixed with Blood** – 1/3 of trees and grass burned.
2. **The Burning Mountain** – 1/3 of the sea turns to blood.
3. **Wormwood** – Freshwater becomes poisoned.
4. **Darkness** – 1/3 of the sun, moon, and stars darkened.
5. **Demonic Locusts** – Tormenting for five months.
6. **The Four Angels Released** – 1/3 of mankind killed.
7. **The Kingdom Declared** – The reign of Christ announced.

The Seven Bowls of Wrath (Revelation 16)

1. **Painful Sores** – Afflicting those with the Mark of the Beast.
2. **The Sea Turns to Blood** – Every living creature in the sea dies.
3. **Freshwater Becomes Blood** – Rivers and springs are undrinkable.
4. **The Sun Scorches the Earth** – People burned with fire.
5. **Darkness Over the Beast's Kingdom** – Pain and suffering increase.
6. **The Euphrates Dries Up** – Armies prepare for Armageddon.
7. **The Greatest Earthquake Ever** – Cities collapse, and judgment is complete.

This timeline confirms the intensity of God's wrath—but believers are taken before it begins!

These appendices provide **a deeper understanding of biblical prophecy**, helping to confirm that:

The 7,000-Year Plan is reaching its fulfillment.
The Rapture happens before the Tribulation.
The Second Coming is separate from the Rapture.
The world is rapidly heading toward judgment.

The question remains—Are you ready?

ACKNOWLEDGMENTS

First and foremost, I want to thank **you, the reader**. Whether this is your first time studying biblical prophecy or you are already well-versed in these truths, I am deeply grateful that you have taken the time to explore this book.

To those who have prayed, encouraged, and supported me in this journey—your faithfulness has been invaluable. Writing this book has been an act of both passion and obedience, and I could not have done it without the strength and wisdom that God has provided.

To my family, who has shaped my faith and given me a firm foundation—I am forever thankful.

To my son, who is searching for truth in a world full of voices—I pray that this book serves as a guide for you, just as Scripture has been for me. May you always find your answers in **God's Word** and stand firm in the foundation that has been instilled in you.

Finally, I acknowledge the **ultimate Author, the One who holds all things together**—our Lord and Savior, Jesus Christ. This book is nothing without **Him**, and it is my deepest hope that every word written here draws you closer to **His truth, His plan, and His soon return.**

Thank you for being a part of this journey.

CALL TO ACTION: SHARE THE MESSAGE, BE PREPARED

We are living in extraordinary times. Prophecy is being fulfilled before our very eyes, and the return of Christ is nearer than ever. The 7,000-year timeline is reaching its conclusion, and the final moments of history are unfolding.

This book was written not just to inform—but to **prepare**.

I challenge you:

Stay Watchful – Keep your heart and mind focused on **God's Word** (Matthew 24:42).

Study the Scriptures for Yourself – Do not rely solely on what you read here—seek **truth directly from the Bible** (Acts 17:11).

Share the Gospel – There are people around you who may never pick up a Bible—but they will listen to **you**. Speak the truth in love (2 Timothy 4:2).

Be Ready – The Lord is coming soon. Make sure your heart is prepared (Revelation 22:12).

If This Book Has Encouraged Or Impacted You, I Invite You To:

Share it with others – Help spread the message of biblical prophecy.

Leave a review – Your thoughts and insights can encourage others to read and learn.

Pray for wisdom and discernment – God promises to guide those who seek Him (James 1:5).

The Spirit and the Bride say, **"Come!"** (Revelation 22:17).

The King is coming. Are you ready?

ABOUT THE AUTHOR

Eric Alger

Eric Christopher Alger is an author, digital strategist, and theological researcher with a deep passion for exploring themes of faith, redemption, and biblical prophecy.

Through his writing, Eric bridges historical and prophetic biblical concepts, offering fresh insights that encourage both personal reflection and group discussion. His works are crafted to help readers uncover the deeper layers of meaning in Scripture, illuminating timeless truths in a new light.

In addition to his writing, Eric is a leader in AI, analytics, and digital marketing, where he merges technology with storytelling to create impactful content. Whether through theological exploration, narrative-driven storytelling, or digital innovation, his mission is consistent: to share knowledge, challenge perspectives, and inspire meaningful transformation.

BOOKS BY THIS AUTHOR

The Eternal Trees: Unveiling The Symbolism Of The Tree Of Life And The Tree Of Knowledge In Scripture

Embark on a transformative journey through Scripture with The Eternal Trees. This insightful study guide delves deep into the symbolism of the Tree of Life and the Tree of Knowledge, tracing their significance from the Garden of Eden to the New Jerusalem. Discover how these ancient symbols reveal profound truths about Christ, eternal life, and the spiritual battle that shapes our lives.

Perfect for Bible study groups, small groups, or personal reflection, The Eternal Trees combines thoughtful commentary with engaging study questions that encourage meaningful discussion and deeper understanding. Whether you're looking to enrich your personal faith journey or seeking fresh material for group study, this book will inspire you to see the Scriptures in a new light and draw closer to God's eternal promises.

Joseph: A Type Of The 6Th Seal And The Feasts

Joseph: A Type of the 6th Seal and the Feasts unveils the profound and timeless story of Joseph, weaving together themes of family, forgiveness, and prophecy. This illuminating exploration reveals Joseph not only as a beloved son and faithful leader but also as a prophetic figure whose life mirrors the 6th Seal in the Book of Revelation. Through each chapter, readers are invited into a deeper understanding of how Joseph's journey connects to the Jewish feasts—especially the Feasts of Trumpets and Atonement—showing how these ancient celebrations foreshadow God's ultimate plan of redemption.

Drawing connections between the Old and New Testaments, this book presents a unique lens on Joseph's life, offering fresh insights into his trials, triumphs, and the enduring legacy he left for all generations. Rich in theological reflections, historical context, and thought-provoking study questions, this book invites readers to journey with Joseph and discover the faith, endurance, and divine purpose that sustained him. Perfect for readers seeking biblical prophecy, historical depth, and spiritual growth, this exploration of Joseph's life is both an educational and transformative experience.

Of Him

We live in a culture obsessed with self-definition—one that tells you to chase your own truth, craft your own identity, and live however you want. But here's the reality: you were created by Him, for Him, and your highest calling is to be one with Him.

This isn't just another theological book—it's a wake-up call. The Bible isn't a collection of disconnected stories; it's a love story, one that begins in Genesis, is fulfilled at the Cross, and culminates in the greatest union in history—the marriage of the Lamb.

In this book, you will:
☐ See how Eve's creation from Adam's side mirrors the Church's birth from Christ's pierced side.
☐ Understand why the Bride must be set apart—clothed in righteousness, washed in His blood, and unspotted by the world.
☐ Explore how ancient Jewish wedding traditions directly foreshadow Christ's return for His Bride.
☐ Discover how every book of the Bible ties into God's eternal plan

to unite Christ with His people.

The Church is not meant to be passive—it is meant to stand firm, prepared, and unshaken in a world that wants to redefine everything. The Bridegroom is coming, and the question isn't whether He is ready for us, but whether we are ready for Him.

Are you willing to reject the lies, reclaim the truth, and step into the love story written before time began?

A Journey To Easter: A Grandpa Joe Story (Series)

The Journey Didn't End at Christmas... It Was Only the Beginning.

The wind rustled through the old oak tree as Grandpa Joe settled by the fire, ready to share another story with his grandchildren, Danny and Hannah. Last year, they discovered the wonder of Christmas—God's promises fulfilled in a manger, love revealed in unexpected places, and hope born under a star. But now, with winter melting into spring, a new story awaits.

This time, it's not just a tale told by the fire—it's an adventure across oceans and centuries.

"We're going to Israel," Grandpa Joe announces. "To walk where Jesus walked. To see where He lived, taught, suffered... and rose again."

What follows is a 40-day journey through the Holy Land, perfectly aligned with the season of Lent. From Bethlehem to Galilee, from Gethsemane to the empty tomb, Grandpa Joe leads Danny and Hannah through the heart of the Gospel—where faith deepens, questions unfold, and Jesus' love is experienced in life-changing ways.

Whether young or old, this story will invite you to reflect, repent, and rejoice—not just on Easter morning, but through every step that leads to it.

This book is for anyone longing to experience Easter in a fresh, powerful way. Step into the sandals of a faithful guide and two curious children as they discover that God's redemptive plan is not just a story from long ago—it's an invitation to walk with Jesus today.

Are you ready to begin the journey?

3 Temples: Types And Shadows

In Three Temples: Types and Shadows, Eric Alger takes readers on a profound theological journey, unraveling the rich prophetic significance of Israel's three temples—Solomon's Temple, the Second Temple, and the anticipated future Temple. Each temple, with its sacred rituals and divine presence, is not only a historical structure but a symbol, or "type," pointing to deeper spiritual truths about Christ and His Church.

Through careful biblical exploration, Alger demonstrates how these physical places of worship prefigure the ultimate reality: the indwelling of the Holy Spirit in the hearts of believers. Each temple, with its unique history and purpose, lays the groundwork for understanding the fulfillment of God's eternal plan—a plan that climaxes in the person of Jesus Christ, who becomes the ultimate Temple.

The book delves deeply into the concept of typology—how the Old Testament temples serve as prophetic foreshadows of Christ's redemptive work. As Alger unveils the Old Testament's rich symbolism, readers will see how these ancient structures and their associated rituals point forward to the New Covenant, where Christ, as the perfect Temple, establishes a new relationship with God's people.

More than just a theological analysis, Three Temples invites readers into a deeper understanding of God's transformative plan for humanity. As the Church—His Bride—is prepared for eternal union with Christ, this book offers invaluable insights into the continuity between the Old and New Testaments, exploring how God's prophetic design is woven throughout Scripture.

Whether you are a theologian, Bible scholar, or a believer eager to understand the full scope of God's redemptive narrative, Three Temples challenges you to explore the timeless truths that run through Scripture. With insightful analysis and scriptural depth, Alger's work is an essential resource for anyone wanting to deepen their understanding of biblical prophecy, typology, and the eternal fulfillment found in Christ and His Church.

Perfect for personal study, group discussions, and anyone seeking to connect the dots of God's grand design, this book will leave you with a renewed sense of awe and purpose as you see the story of salvation unfold through the temples of Israel.

www.ingramcontent.com/pod-product-compliance
Lightning Source LLC
Chambersburg PA
CBHW070752180626
46818CB00007B/3087